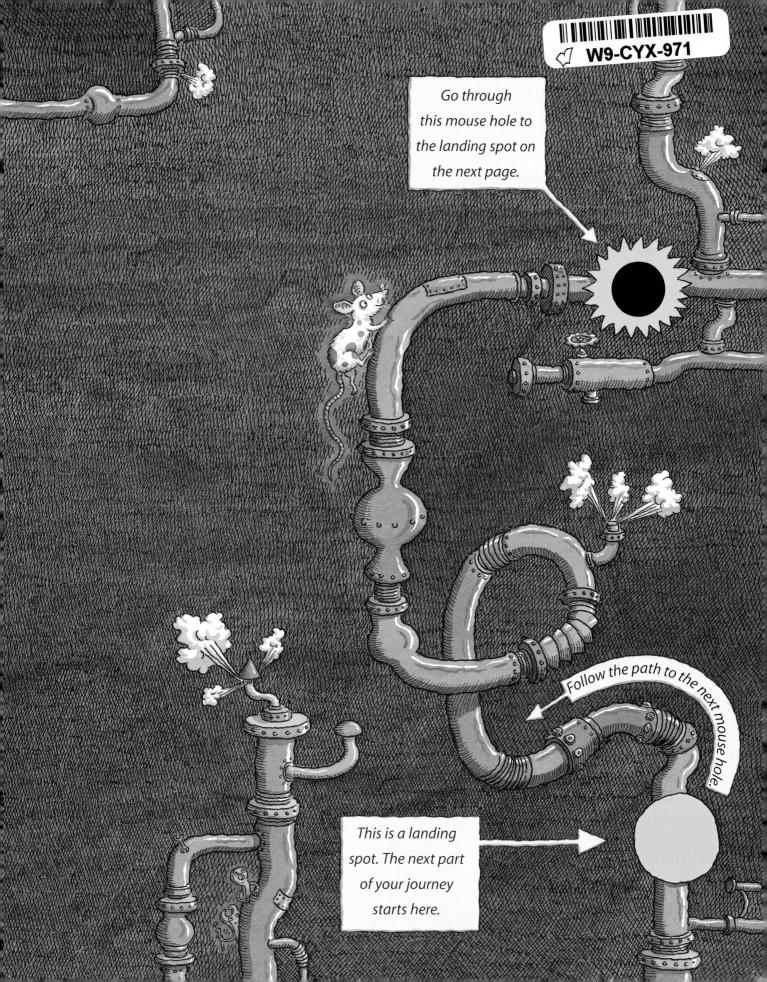

MOUSEMAZIA

AN AMAZING DREAM HOUSE MAZE

ANNA NILSEN

ILLUSTRATED BY
DOM MANSELL

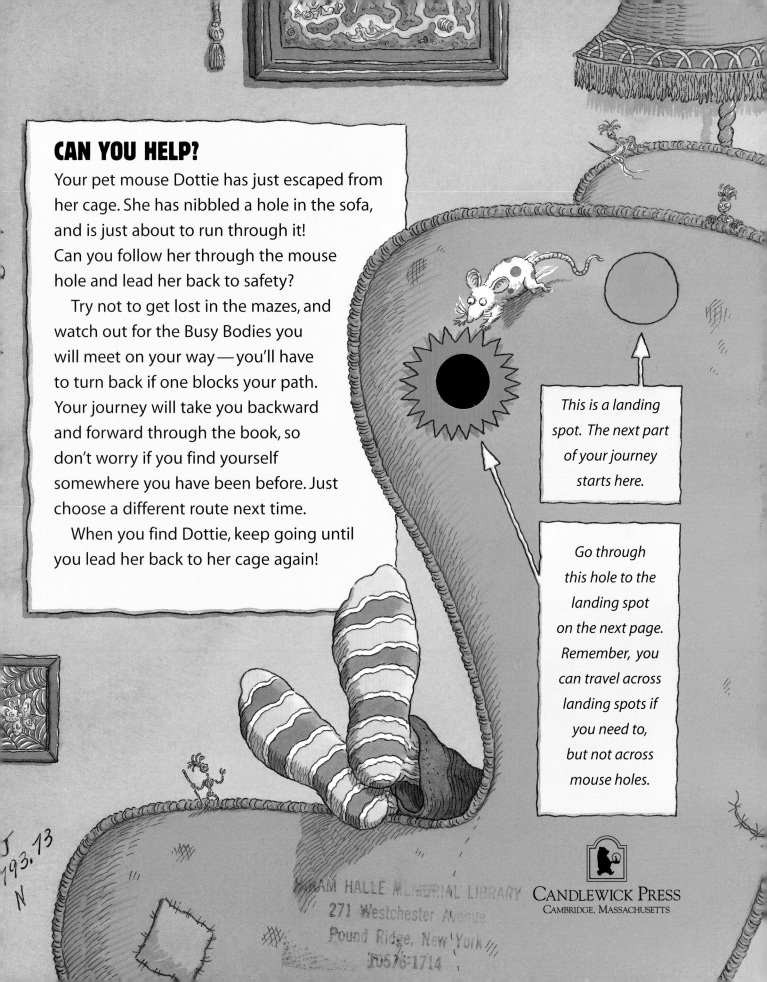

CAN YOU HELP?

Your pet mouse Dottie has just escaped from her cage. She has nibbled a hole in the sofa, and is just about to run through it! Can you follow her through the mouse hole and lead her back to safety?

Try not to get lost in the mazes, and watch out for the Busy Bodies you will meet on your way—you'll have to turn back if one blocks your path. Your journey will take you backward and forward through the book, so don't worry if you find yourself somewhere you have been before. Just choose a different route next time.

When you find Dottie, keep going until you lead her back to her cage again!

This is a landing spot. The next part of your journey starts here.

Go through this hole to the landing spot on the next page. Remember, you can travel across landing spots if you need to, but not across mouse holes.

CANDLEWICK PRESS
CAMBRIDGE, MASSACHUSETTS

SOFA SPRINGS

You are deep inside the sofa! Busy Bodies are cleaning and mending. You must find a way along the springs and ropes to a mouse hole. Remember, if you meet a Busy Body, you'll have to turn back!

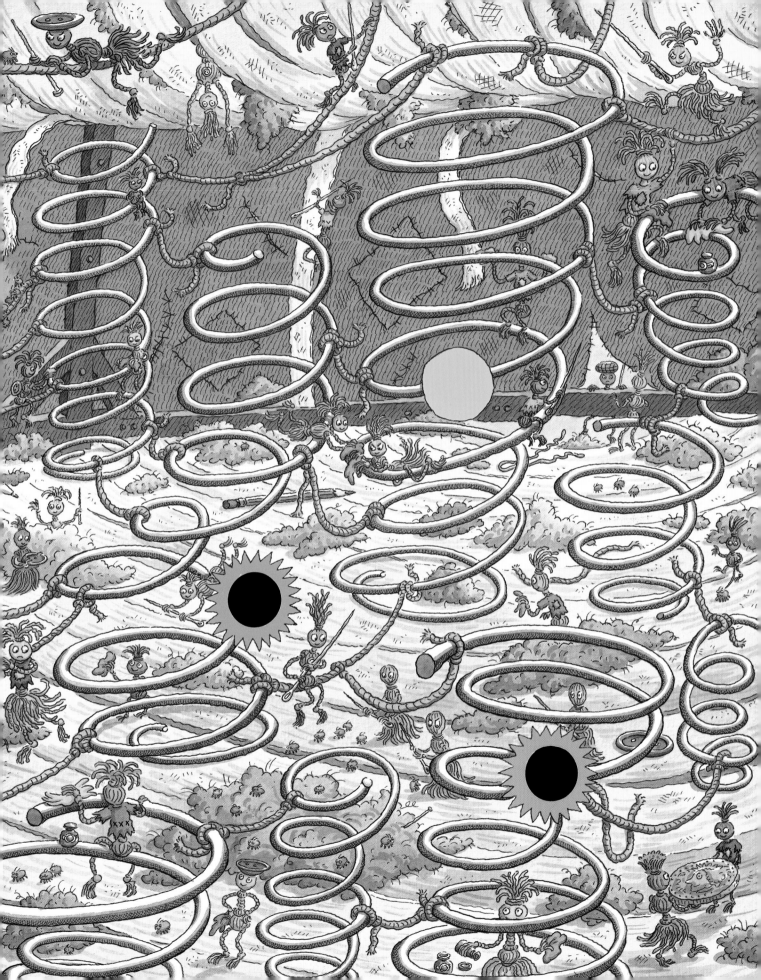

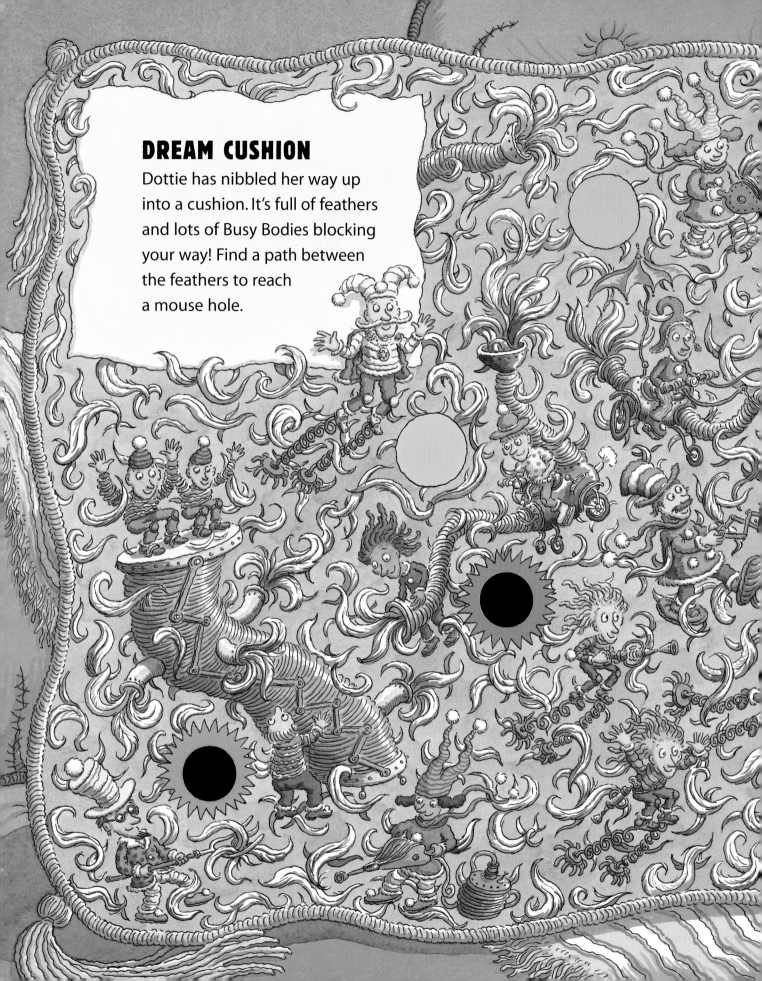

DREAM CUSHION

Dottie has nibbled her way up into a cushion. It's full of feathers and lots of Busy Bodies blocking your way! Find a path between the feathers to reach a mouse hole.

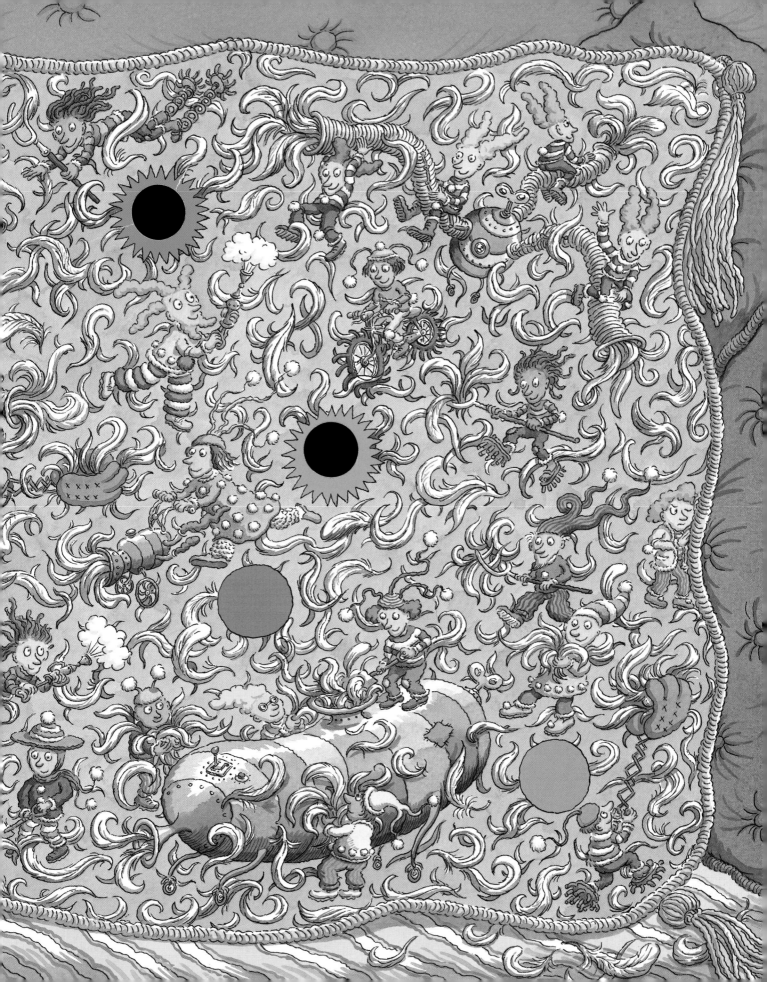

TELEVISION TOWERS

The only way around these television towers deep inside the TV is to travel on the striped wires. Try to avoid the sparking Busy Bodies!

COG CITY

Now you are inside the clock! There are so many wheels and cogs, all whirring and ticking! Find a path along the brass machinery. If you meet one of the Busy Body timekeepers, turn back at once!

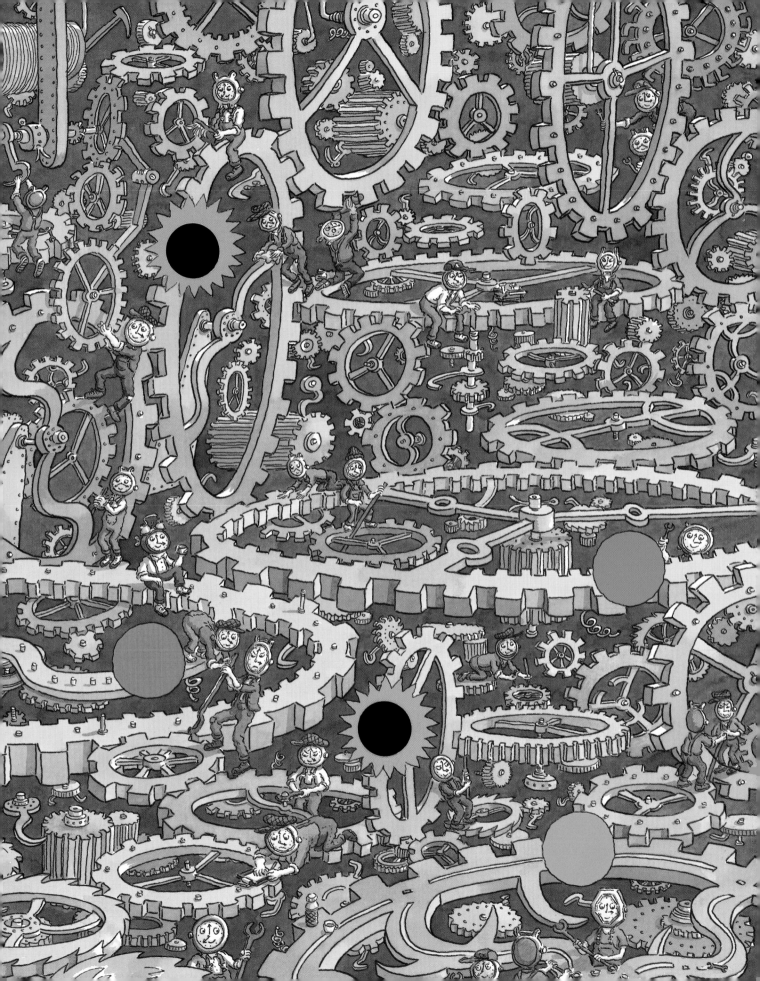

WHISTLING PIPES

Swish! Swoosh! Where are you? Among the heating pipes! Follow the pipes to escape—and be sure to avoid the clouds of steam and the Busy Bodies.

COBWEB CAVERN

Ugh! Webs and spiders everywhere! Look out for the Busy Bodies, too. To get out, find an unblocked path along the webs. Good luck!

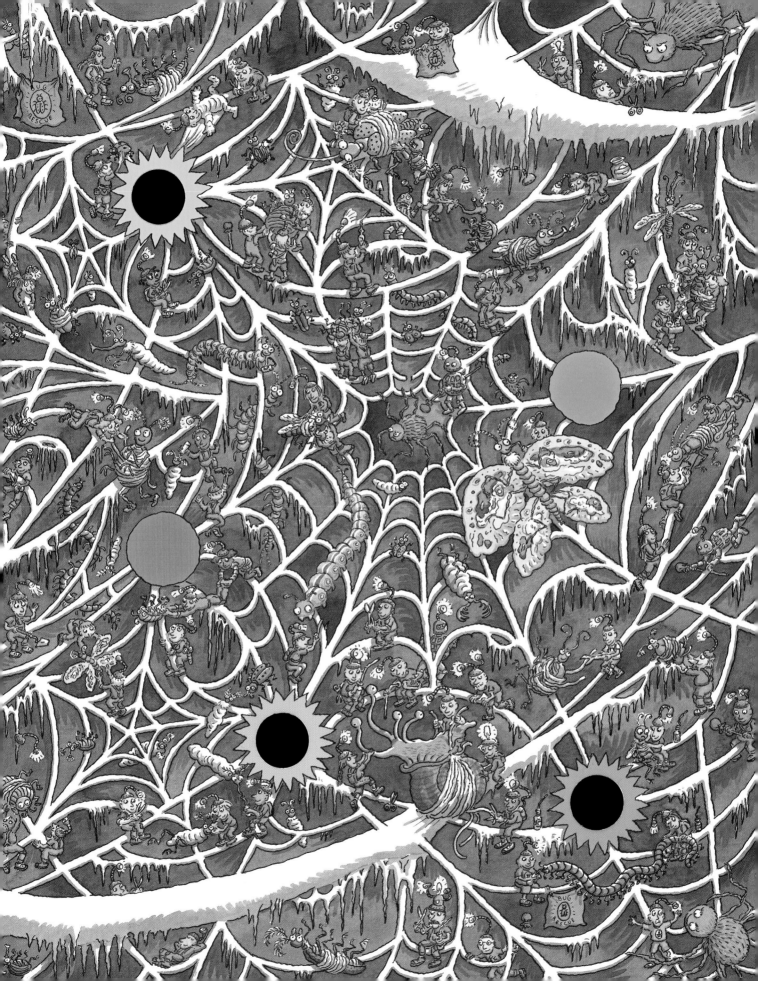

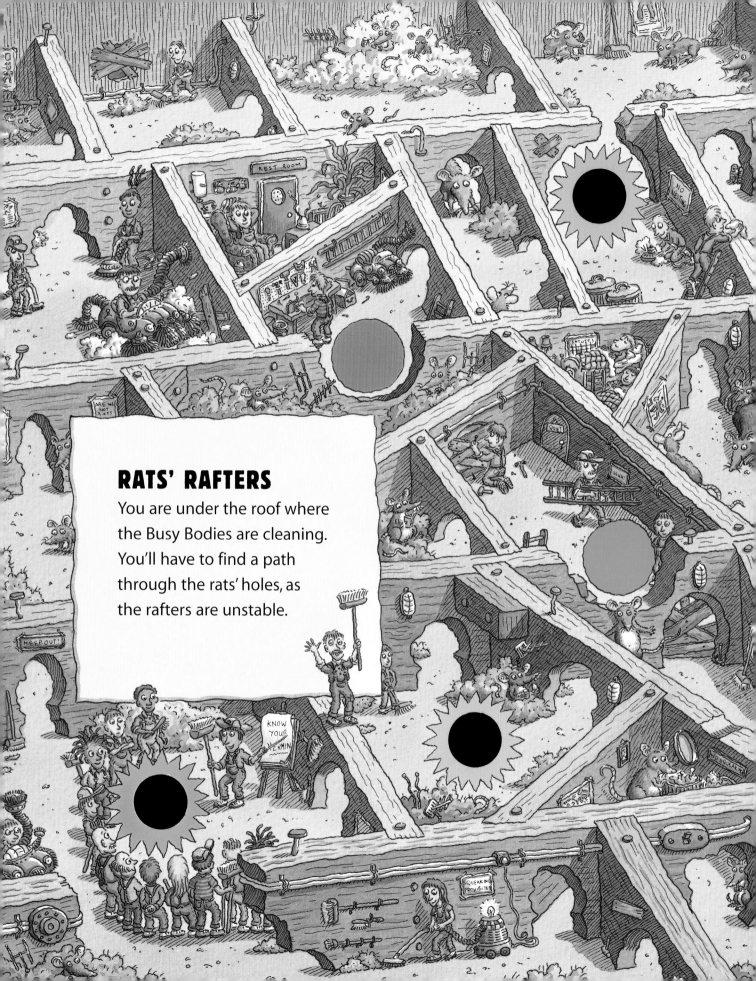

RATS' RAFTERS

You are under the roof where the Busy Bodies are cleaning. You'll have to find a path through the rats' holes, as the rafters are unstable.

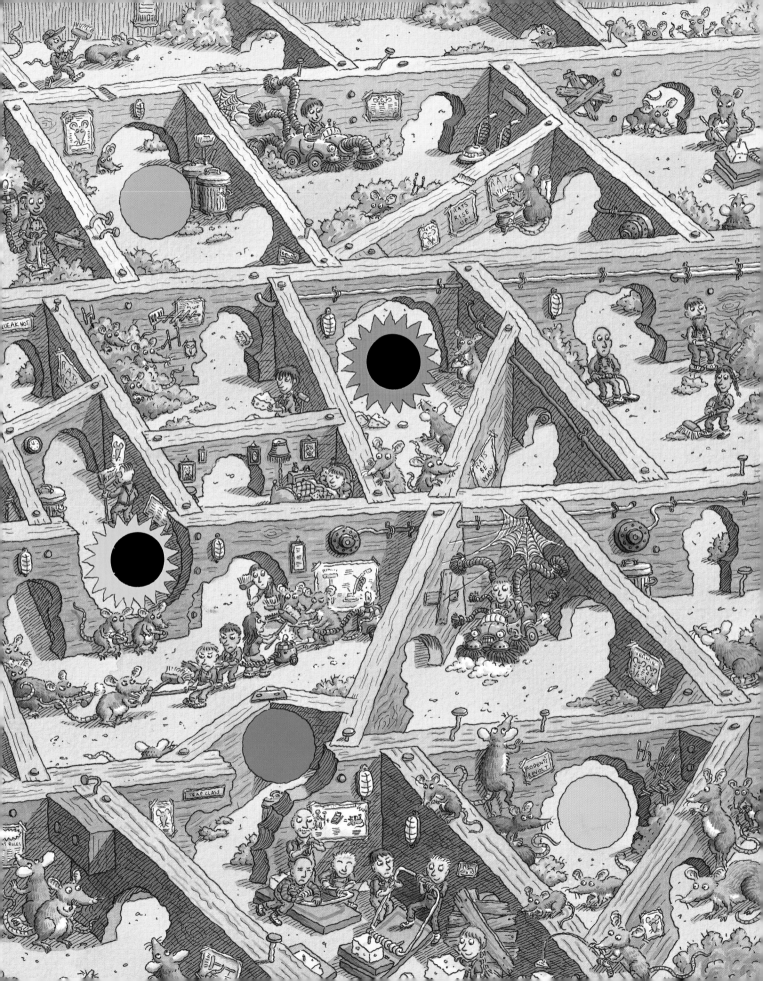

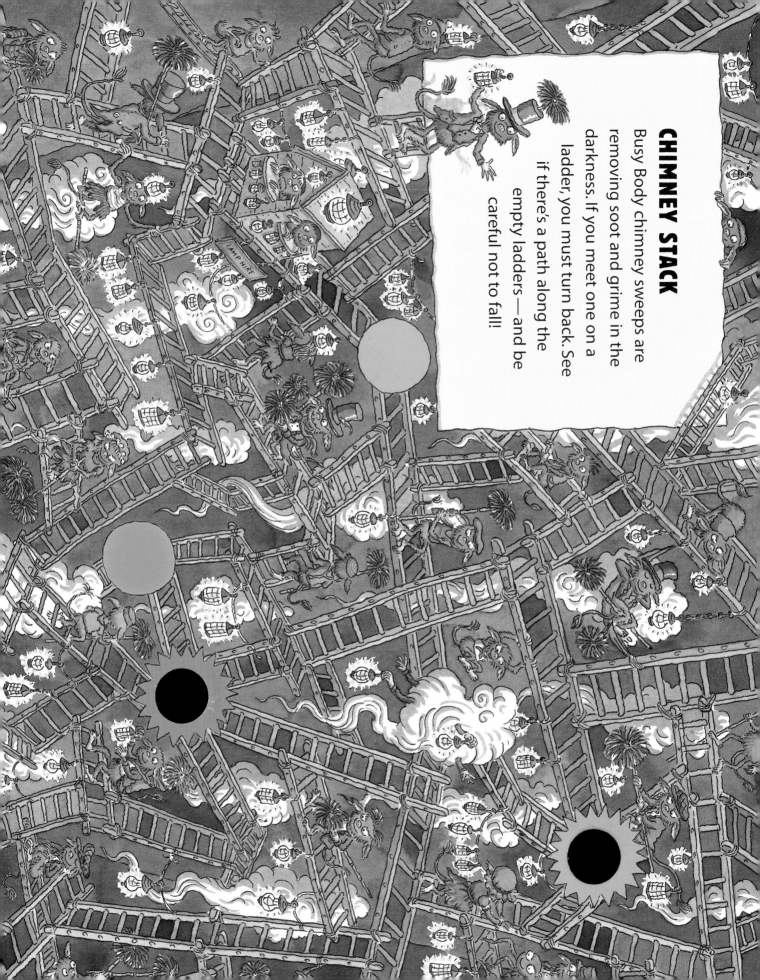

CHIMNEY STACK

Busy Body chimney sweeps are removing soot and grime in the darkness. If you meet one on a ladder, you must turn back. See if there's a path along the empty ladders—and be careful not to fall!

ROOF

Here you are up in the sky! The roof tiles are slippery with moss and covered with Busy Body cleaners. Find a clear path across the tiles to get safely off this roof.

CLINGING IVY

How can you get to the ground again? The Busy Bodies are all over the wall—snipping off dead leaves, cleaning up snail trails, and watering. Find a way down to the ground by following the stems up, down, and around. Stay away from the slippery leaves!

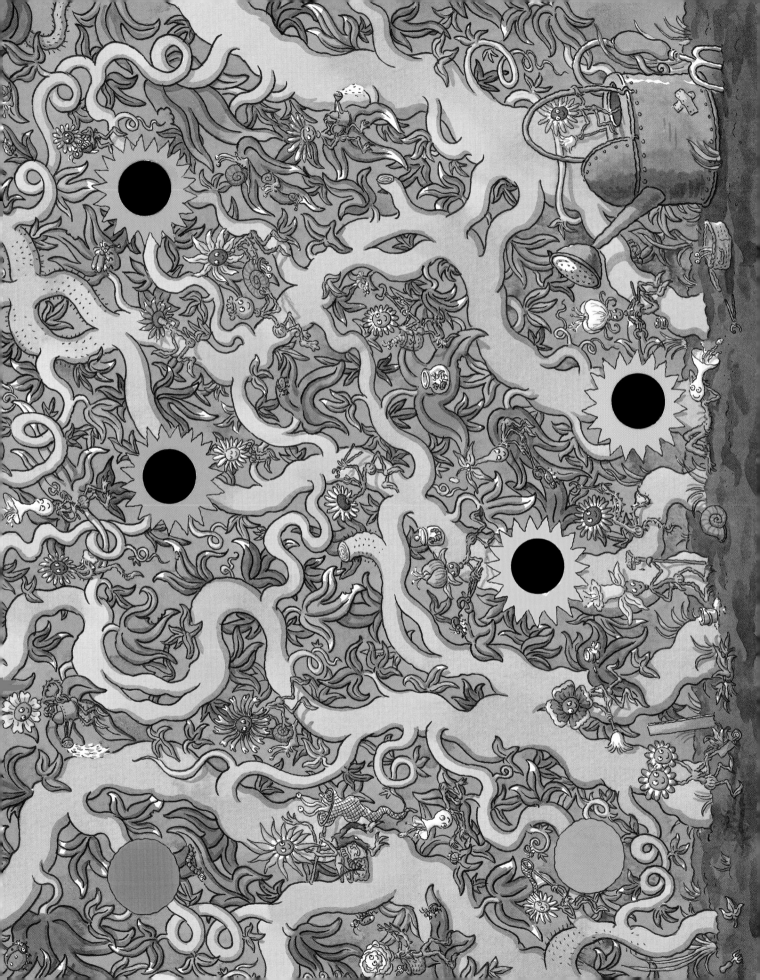

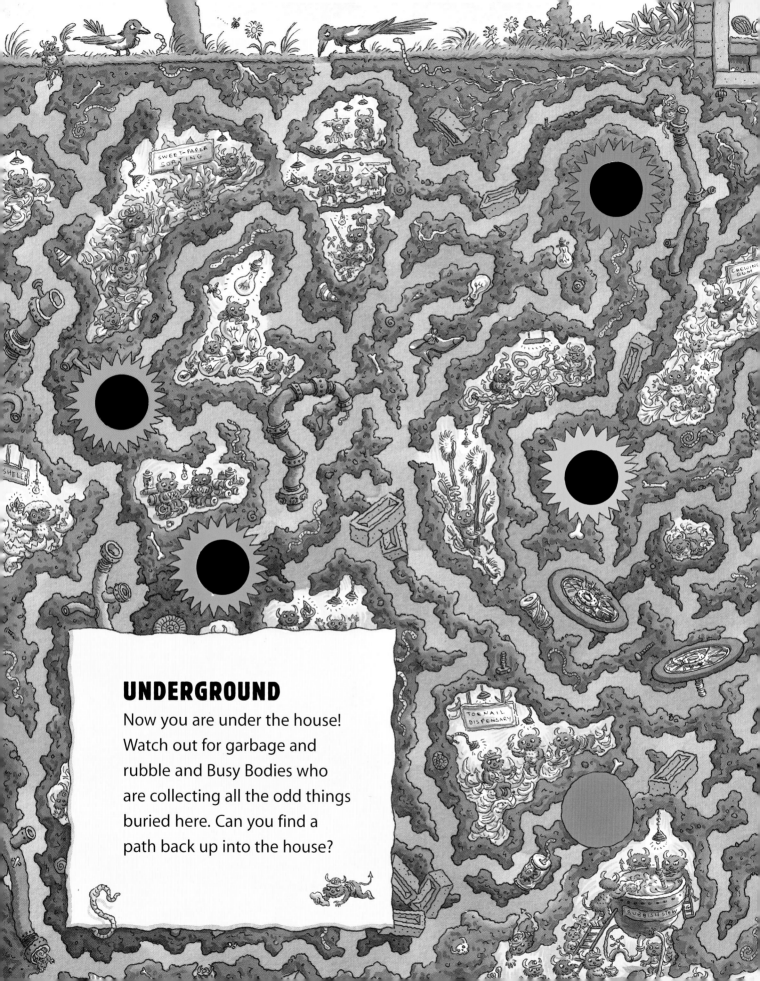

UNDERGROUND

Now you are under the house! Watch out for garbage and rubble and Busy Bodies who are collecting all the odd things buried here. Can you find a path back up into the house?

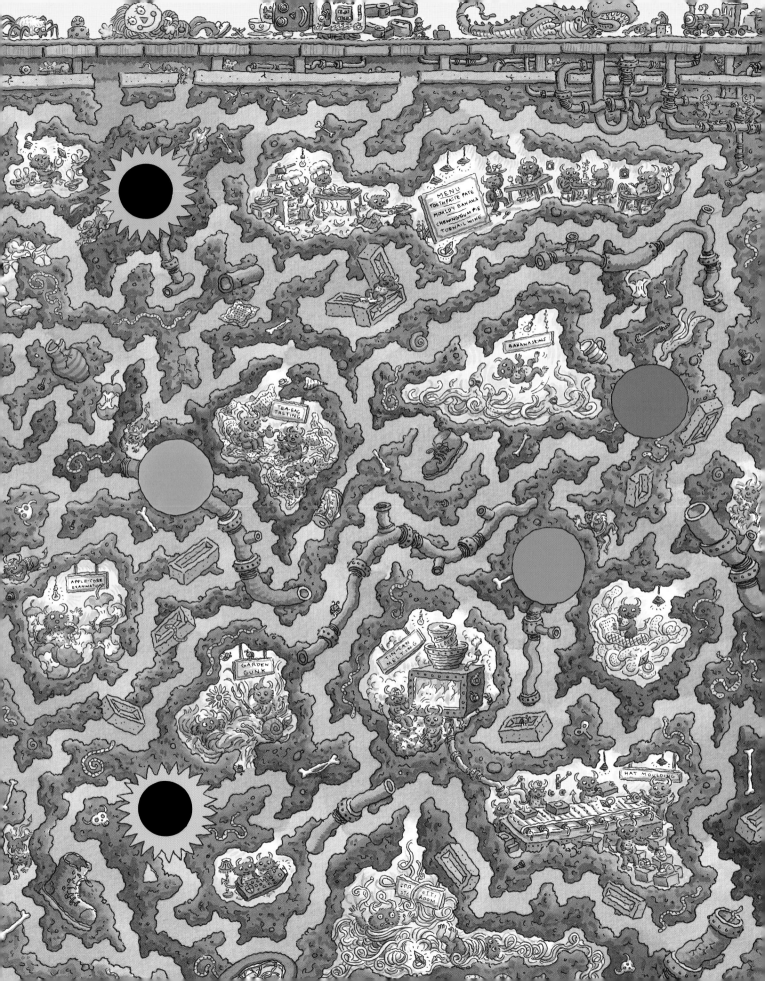

PLAYROOM

Good job! You have led Dottie back to her cage.

But wait! Dottie knocked over the jewelry box, and ten rings have been lost. First find the ruby ring in this room, then trace a path from it to the dark hole in the floor. Go through the hole and find nine emerald rings under the house. Then take them back to the jewelry box — your journey is finally over!

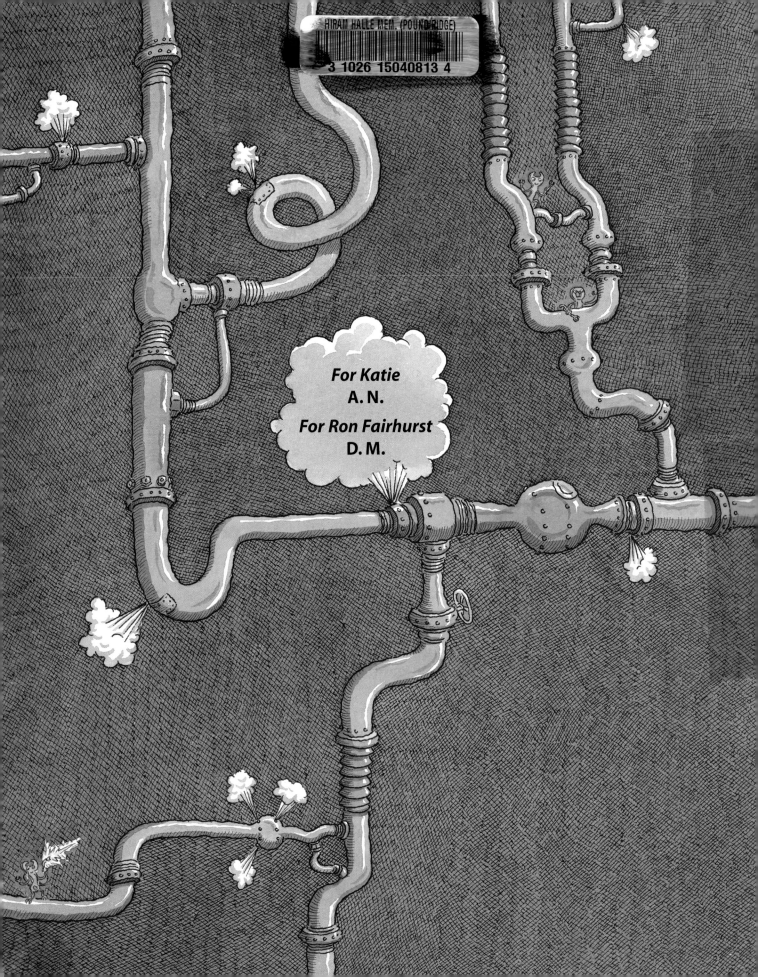

For Katie
A. N.

For Ron Fairhurst
D. M.